D1437100

The Same But
DIFFERENT

EMER O'NEILL
Illustrated by Debby Rahmalia

GILL BOOKS

EMER O'NEILL is a mother of two. Born and raised in Ireland, she is Irish-Nigerian and a Bray, Co.Wicklow, native. She teaches Physical Education and is the Transition Year Coordinator at North Wicklow Secondary School. She is a presenter on RTÉ Home School Hub. Emer is well known as an anti-racism activist and as an advocate for positive body image.

DEBBY RAHMALIA is from Indonesia. She graduated from Bandung Institute of Technology, where she earned a Bachelor of Interior Design degree. Having always loved children's books, she became an illustrator after her first child was born.

DUDLEY LIBRARIES	
000003105353	
Askews & Holts	18-Oct-2021
JF PIC	£12.99
2CR	

Dedicated to Sunny Rae and Kyan.
Remember that being different is not a
barrier – it is a beautiful thing.

With love from Mom x

Once there was a girl named Emer, as cute as cute could be,
Full of fun and mischief and playfulness and glee.

But as she grew up she often wondered why
Some people stared at her and sometimes made her cry.

She realised her skin was brown and not like all her friends'.

Her hair was thick
and curly and frizzy
at the ends.

The other children called her names and made her feel so bad.

She wished that she could look like them and have the hair they had.

They'd say, 'Hey, can we touch your hair?' and 'You have funny skin!'

This really hurt her and made her sad within.

Her mum would say, 'You're beautiful, talented and smart.'
But still Emer felt sad deep inside her heart.

Her mum said, 'Look at all the crayons in your pencil case.'

'So many different colours
make the world a nicer place.'

'If we all looked just the same how boring life would be. The things that make me different are the things that make me *me*!'

She decided to ignore the hurt that people tried to cause –

Instead she learned to love herself just the way she was.

The moral of the story is we should always just be kind

And look beyond a person's skin to what is in their mind.

We should love our differences, whatever they may be,

Be happy being who we are and let our spirits free.

Even with our differences we are all just the same,
Running, jumping, having fun and playing lots of games.

It's nice to treat each other with kindness and respect,
To love one another, and find ways to connect.

Now Emer is happy, because this time she knows

We're all the same but different, and that is how life goes!

Gill Books
Hume Avenue
Park West
Dublin 12
www.gillbooks.ie
Gill Books is an imprint of M.H. Gill and Co.

Text © Emer O'Neill
Illustrations © Debby Rahmalia
9780717192854

Designed by www.grahamthew.com
Printed by Printed by Hussar Books, Poland

This book is typeset in 20pt New Spirit
The paper used in this book comes from the wood pulp of managed forests. For every
tree felled, at least one tree is planted, thereby renewing natural resources.
All rights reserved.
No part of this publication may be copied, reproduced or transmitted in any form or
by any means, without written permission of the publishers.
A CIP catalogue record for this book is available from the British Library.
5 4 3 2 1